Color Me
CHRISTMAS

Color Me Christmas for Kids!

13-Digit ISBN: 978-1-40034-679-0
10-Digit ISBN: 1-40034-679-7

This book may be ordered by mail from the publisher. Please include $5.99 for postage and handling. Please support your local bookseller first!

Books published by Cider Mill Press Book Publishers are available at special discounts for bulk purchases in the United States by corporations, institutions, and other organizations. For more information, please contact the publisher.

Cider Mill Press Book Publishers
"Where Good Books Are Ready for Press"
501 Nelson Place
Nashville, Tennessee 37214

cidermillpress.com

Typography: Epicursive Script, Filson Pro, PeachyKeenJF, Catseye

Printed in the USA

24 25 26 27 28 VER 6 5 4 3 2

Color Me CHRISTMAS

FOR KIDS!

30 Festive Coloring Pages

Illustrations by Ela Jarząbek

Introduction

Did you know that coloring is scientifically proven to make you feel happier and more relaxed? It's true! And we don't have any data to back this up, but we're willing to bet that goes double for Christmas coloring books. Because who doesn't love Christmas? This coloring book is filled with classic Christmas scenes, from Santa flying across the sky with his reindeer to kittens getting cozy under the tree.

These incredible illustrations are meant for artists of all ages and skill levels. The pages are one-sided, so your art won't bleed through. You can use whatever tool you want to fill in these delightful designs: colored pencils, markers, gel pens, watercolors, crayons, you name it. Color inside the lines or outside of them—the point is to relax and create something that makes you happy.

Be proud of your work! As long as you have fun, your coloring will bring joy to anyone who sees it. Share your creations with the world by posting on social media (with your parents' permission!) using the hashtag #colormechristmas, and be sure to tag us @cidermillpress! 'Tis the season for coloring with *Color Me Christmas (for Kids!)*.

About
APPLESAUCE PRESS
BOOK PUBLISHERS

Good ideas ripen with time. From seed to harvest, Applesauce Press crafts books with beautiful designs, creative formats, and kid-friendly information on a variety of topics. Like our parent company, Cider Mill Press Book Publishers, our press bears fruit twice a year, publishing a new crop of titles each spring and fall.

"Where Good Books Are Ready for Press"

501 Nelson Place
Nashville, Tennessee 37214

cidermillpress.com